T0001553

This book belongs to

....

For Freya.
MB

To Max, lots of love, Gwen (Mom) x

With thanks to child psychotherapist Sarah Davis
for her support and guidance.

SOMETIMES I'M A BABY BEAR, SOMETIMES I'M A SNAIL

Published in 2022 by Welbeck Editions
An imprint of Welbeck Children's Limited, part of Welbeck Publishing Group.
Based in London and Sydney.
www.welbeckpublishing.com

Design and layout © Welbeck Children's Limited 2022
Text © Moira Butterfield 2022
Illustration © Gwen Millward 2022

Moira Butterfield and Gwen Millward have asserted their moral rights to be identified as the author and illustrator of this Work in accordance with the Copyright Designs and Patents Act 1988.

Consultant: Sarah Davis, UKCP registered child psychotherapist
Associate Publisher: Laura Knowles
Art Editor: Deborah Vickers

All rights reserved. No part of this publication may be reproduced, stored in a retrieval system, or transmitted in any form or by any means, electronically, mechanical, photocopying, recording or otherwise, without the prior permission of the copyright owners and the publishers.

ISBN 978 1 80338 018 6

Printed in Donguan, China

10 9 8 7 6 5 4 3 2 1

FSC
www.fsc.org
MIX
Paper from
responsible sources
FSC® C144853

SOMETIMES I'M A BABY BEAR, SOMETIMES I'M A SNAIL

Moira Butterfield

Illustrated by Gwen Millward

WELBECK
EDITIONS

Sometimes I'm a bouncy **puppy**.
I feel like playing with everyone,
joining in and having fun.

Today's a day when I want to play!

Sometimes I'm a **snail** inside my shell.
I'd rather be quiet and on my own.
I'm fine playing games alone.

Sometimes my friend is a **snail**, too.
She wants to be quiet. That's OK.
I'll play with her another day.

Sometimes I'm a baby **bear**
who loves getting big hugs.
Do I want a cuddly squeeze?
Yes please!

Hurrah! It's a bear-hug day!

Sometimes I'm a no-hug **bird.**
I'd rather stay in my tree.
Right now a hug is not for me.

It's fine, by the way,
to feel this way!

Sometimes my friend is a no-hug **bird.**
She doesn't want cuddles and that's OK.
We'll have our hugs another day.

Sometimes, instead of giving hugs,
I'd rather be a **blowfish**.
I'll blow you a kiss, just like this.

Here comes my kiss. Catch!

Sometimes I'm a fearless **lion.**
I feel as brave as brave can be.
Everybody, look at me!

I feel like I can do anything when I'm a lion.
Roar!

Sometimes I'm a tiny **mouse**.
I feel a little bit scared and shy
about things I'm asked to try.

We all have days when
we feel this way.

Sometimes my friend's a tiny mouse.
She feels shy too, just like I do,
so I tell her something that I try.

I can sometimes change how I feel in my head
by pretending to be a lion instead!

We can be like lots of animals.

Cross like a grumpy gorilla.

Excited like a **dolphin** leaping.

Sad like a **dog** with droopy ears.

If you want to tell someone how you feel
you can say you're like an animal, too ...
a bear, a snail, or a bird maybe,
just like my friend and me!

Today we're both happy cats.
Prrrrrr!

Using this book

We know that children who can express their feelings are likely to feel less frustrated and will start to grow awareness of the feelings of others. We also want children to have their choices respected and listened to by others. Here are some tips to help you and your child get the most from your reading experience.

It's tough for kids to explain their feelings, especially ones that might possibly be difficult for others to hear—such as "I don't want a hug today" or "I want to play on my own now." Expressing feelings linked to familiar animals will help give children some workable communication tools. Have fun reading this book and encourage your child to act out the feelings of the creatures featured, with noises and miming. Making the time an enjoyable experience will ensure the suggestions will not feel prescriptive or pressurizing.

As you read, discuss how the characters are feeling in the book. Feelings can be positive as well as negative and this book includes both because they are all good to express. No one feeling has been emphasized and dwelled on as something to cause a child pressure.

Refer to the book animals and their feelings in everyday life, so your child becomes familiar with the concept of expressing themselves with phrases such as "I feel sad like the dog with droopy ears in my book" or "I'd like to be the no-hug bird today." Make sure you give your child positive acknowledgement when they express their feelings in this way.

You could also mention other alternatives for not hugging, such as doing a high-five or a fist bump. Your child might sometimes prefer one of these to blowing a kiss.

The word "shy," expressed as a permanent feeling (such as "she is shy," rather than "she is feeling shy"), can unfairly label a child. Encourage the awareness that feelings change, so that children become used to the idea that they're not "stuck" with a feeling.

The book links a child's feelings to those of a friend, to help them understand and draw comfort from the fact that others share similar feelings to them. At an age when their peer relationships start to take on a deeper meaning, this can really enrich interactions with their widening social circle.